The Last Heir: A Family Legacy

Christopher Reed

Published by RWG Publishing, 2023.

This is a work of fiction. Similarities to real people, places, or events are entirely coincidental.

THE LAST HEIR: A FAMILY LEGACY

First edition. January 26, 2023.

Written by Christopher Reed.

Table of Contents

Chapter 1: Introduction

The sun was setting over the city, casting a warm orange glow over the bustling streets below. In a grand, old mansion on the outskirts of town, a young woman sat alone in a dimly lit room, staring blankly at the envelope in her hands. Her name, written in bold, elegant script, stared back at her from the front of the envelope. With a trembling hand, she tore it open and pulled out the letter inside.

"Dear Miss Wilson,

We regret to inform you of the passing of your father, Jack Wilson, the last remaining member of the Wilson family. As his only living heir, it is with great sadness that we inform you of your inheritance of the Wilson fortune and estate.

Please report to our offices at your earliest convenience to discuss the details of your inheritance and the responsibilities that come with it.

Sincerely,

Jim Martin, Martin Law Firm

The young woman couldn't believe what she was reading. Her father, who she had never met, had passed away, leaving her the last heir of a powerful and wealthy family. She had always known that her father was from a wealthy family, but she had never imagined that she would one day inherit their fortune.

As she sat there, reading the letter over and over again, she couldn't help but feel a mix of emotions. On one hand, she was excited at the prospect of inheriting such a vast fortune and all that came with it. On the other hand, she was terrified at the thought of the responsibilities and expectations that would come with it. She knew that inheriting the Wilson fortune would change her life forever, and she wasn't quite sure if she was ready for it.

With a deep sigh, the young woman folded the letter and tucked it back into the envelope. She knew that there was no turning back now, and that she would have to face the responsibilities of being the last heir of the Wilson family head on.

As she left her small apartment and headed to the offices of Martin Law Firm, she couldn't help but wonder what the future held for her and the Wilson family. She was about to find out that being the last heir was not as easy as she thought and that it will come with sacrifices and consequences.

Chapter 2: The Family History

The young woman, now the last heir of the Wilson family, sat in the conference room of Marin Law Firm, surrounded by lawyers and advisors, as they explained the details of her inheritance. As they spoke, she couldn't help but feel a sense of overwhelming responsibility and pressure.

But as they delved deeper into the history of the Wilson family, she began to understand the weight of her inheritance. The Wilson family had been one of the wealthiest and most powerful families in the city for generations. They had built their fortune through a combination of savvy business dealings and strategic investments. But it wasn't just their wealth that made them powerful, it was also the influence they wielded in the city's political and social circles.

The young woman listened as they spoke of her ancestors, who had been pioneers in industry, philanthropists, and even politicians. They had left a lasting legacy in the city and had a hand in shaping its history. But as the years passed, the family's power and influence began to wane, and the number of heirs began to dwindle.

Now, with her father's passing, she was the last remaining member of the Wilson family, and the responsibility of maintaining their legacy and fortune fell solely on her shoulders. She couldn't help but feel a sense of awe and reverence for her ancestors and the legacy they had built, but also a sense of fear and uncertainty about whether she was capable of living up to their legacy.

As she left the offices of Martin Law Firm, her head was spinning with the new information. She knew that in order to fully understand her inheritance and the responsibilities that came with it, she would have to delve deeper into her family's history. She decided to take a tour of the Wilson estate and visit the places where her ancestors had lived and worked.

As she walked through the grand halls and rooms of the estate, she felt a sense of connection to her ancestors and their legacy. She saw the portraits of her family members hanging on the walls, and she couldn't help but wonder about their lives, their dreams, and their struggles. She knew that in order to truly understand her inheritance and live up to her ancestors' legacy, she would have to uncover the truth about her family's history, good and bad.

In the following chapters, she will uncover secrets, betrayals and hidden agendas that shape the course of her journey to understand her family's history and her inheritance.

Chapter 3: The Will

The young woman, the last heir of the Wilson family, sat in the conference room of Martin Law Firm, surrounded by her father's advisors and lawyers, as they presented her with the last will and testament of her father. The room was silent as she began to read the document, her eyes scanning the pages for any clues about her inheritance and the responsibilities that came with it.

As she read through the will, she quickly realized that her father had not left her the fortune and the estate outright. Instead, he had set up a series of conditions that she must meet in order to inherit the fortune. These conditions included taking over the management of the family's businesses within a year, maintaining the family's philanthropic efforts and charitable foundations, and preserving the family's legacy.

The young woman couldn't help but feel a sense of frustration and anger as she read through the will. She had never met her father, and now he was dictating the terms of her inheritance from beyond the grave. She wondered why he never reached out to her before, why he left her to figure everything out by herself.

But as she continued to read, she realized that her father had not set these conditions to be cruel or controlling, but to ensure that the Wilson fortune and legacy would be preserved for future generations. He wanted to make sure that the family's wealth and influence would be used for good and that the family's legacy would continue to be upheld. He had put in place a series of tests to ensure that the heir was worthy and capable of taking on the responsibility.

As she looked up from the will, the young woman knew that she had a lot of work ahead of her. She would have to take over the management of the family's businesses, learn about the philanthropic efforts that the family had been involved in, and find a way to preserve the family's legacy. She realized that inheriting the Wilson fortune was not just about the money, but about fulfilling her responsibilities as the last heir of the family.

The advisors and lawyers explained to her the details of the will, the deadlines and the consequences of not fulfilling the terms. They also offered her their support and resources to help her in her journey.

As she left the conference room, the young woman felt a mix of emotions, she felt overwhelmed by the responsibility, but also determined to fulfill the conditions of the will and inherit the fortune. She knew that it wouldn't be easy, but she was ready to take on the challenge and prove herself as the last heir of the Wilson family.

Chapter 4: The Challenges

The young woman, the last heir of the Wilson family, had spent the past few days trying to come to terms with her inheritance and the responsibilities that came with it. She had read her father's will, spoken with his advisors and lawyers, and was now ready to take on the challenge of fulfilling the conditions of the will.

But as she began to dive deeper into the family's businesses and philanthropic efforts, she quickly realized that the journey ahead would not be an easy one. She faced a number of challenges and obstacles that threatened to derail her plans.

One of the first challenges she faced was opposition from other family members. She soon discovered that not everyone in the family was happy about her inheriting the fortune and some had their own agendas. They saw her as an outsider and resented her taking over the family's businesses and philanthropic efforts. They were willing to do whatever it takes to sabotage her efforts and prevent her from inheriting the fortune. They were also trying to challenge the will and claim the fortune for themselves. Some of them went as far as spreading rumors and lies about her, trying to tarnish her reputation.

Another challenge she faced was the complexity of the family's businesses. She had never been involved in the family's business dealings before, and she quickly realized that she had a lot to learn. She had to familiarize herself with the different companies, their finances, and their operations. Many of the companies were not doing well, they were struggling with debts and declining revenues. She had to make difficult decisions and had to work with a team of managers and advisors to turn the businesses around and make them profitable. She had to make tough choices, some of which involved layoffs and downsizing, which made her unpopular with some of the employees.

The young woman also found that the philanthropic efforts of the family were not as straightforward as she thought. She had to navigate the complex world of non-profits and charitable foundations. She had to learn about the different programs and initiatives that the family had been involved in, such as funding education programs, supporting the arts and healthcare initiatives. She also had to make sure that these initiatives were still relevant and effective, and decide which ones to continue supporting and which ones to discontinue. She faced criticism and backlash from some of the organizations and individuals who relied on the family's funding and support.

As she struggled to keep up with all the challenges and obstacles, she couldn't help but feel overwhelmed and frustrated. She wondered if she was truly ready and capable of fulfilling the conditions of the will and inheriting the fortune.

But as the days passed, she began to realize that the challenges she was facing were not just obstacles to her inheritance, they were also opportunities for her to grow and learn. She knew that she would have to be persistent, resilient, and resourceful to overcome the challenges and fulfill her responsibilities as the last heir of the Wilson family. She also realized that some of the challenges were opportunities to make a positive impact and make a difference in the community. She was determined to prove herself and to live up to her father's expectations and her ancestors' legacy. She knew that it will be a long and hard journey, but she was ready to face the challenges head on.

Chapter 5: The Search for Answers

The young woman, the last heir of the Wilson family, was facing a number of challenges as she tried to fulfill the conditions of her father's will and inherit the fortune. She was dealing with opposition from other family members, struggling to turn around the family's businesses and navigate the complex world of philanthropy.

As she worked to overcome these challenges, she found herself with more questions than answers. She wanted to understand her father's motivations for setting the conditions of the will, and why he had never reached out to her before. She also wanted to know more about her family's history and the legacy that she was supposed to preserve.

So, the young woman decided to go on a search for answers. She knew that in order to fully understand her inheritance and fulfill her responsibilities, she would have to uncover the truth about her family's history.

She began by digging into the family's business dealings, looking for any clues or secrets that her father may have kept hidden. She pored over financial records, interviewed employees, and spoke with her father's business associates. As she delved deeper, she began to uncover a web of lies and deceit that had been hidden for years. She found that some of the businesses were involved in illegal activities, such as money laundering and bribery, which were the reasons for the company's financial struggles.

She also began to learn more about her family's philanthropic efforts. She visited the organizations and initiatives that the family had supported, and spoke with the people who had been impacted by their generosity. As she learned more about the good work that her family had done, she felt a sense of pride and connection to her ancestors and their legacy. However, she also found out that some of the philanthropic efforts were just a cover-up for the illegal activities of the business.

But as she delved deeper into her family's history, she also uncovered a darker side. She learned about the questionable business practices, the secret deals, and the corruption that had been a part of her family's past. She was shocked and saddened by what she discovered. She also found out that her father knew about these activities and had tried to stop it but had failed.

The young woman knew that she had to come to terms with the truth about her family's history, both the good and the bad. She realized that in order to fulfill her responsibilities as the last heir of the Wilson family, she would have to make amends for the mistakes of the past and find a way to continue her ancestors' legacy in a way that was true to her values. She knew that it would not be easy, but she was determined to make things right, she wanted to honor her father's wishes by cleaning up the family's past and ensuring that the family's wealth and influence would be used for good in the future.

As she continues her search for answers, she faces difficult decisions and moral dilemmas. She must decide how to handle the illegal activities of the family's businesses, whether to shut them down or try to reform them. She also must decide how to handle the philanthropic foundations and initiatives that have been tainted by the family's past actions.

The young woman knew that her journey to uncover the truth about her family's history would not be easy, but she was determined to see it through. She knew that understanding the past was crucial to shaping the future and fulfilling her responsibilities as the last heir of the Wilson family. Despite the challenges and difficulties, she was ready to face them head on, with the goal of making her family's legacy a source of pride and inspiration for generations to come.

Chapter 6: The Betrayal

The young woman, the last heir of the Wilson family, had been on a mission to uncover the truth about her family's history and fulfill her responsibilities as the last heir. She had faced many challenges and obstacles, but she was determined to see it through.

However, she was not prepared for the betrayal she encountered. As she was working to turn around the family's struggling businesses and restore the family's reputation, she found out that one of her father's most trusted advisors had been embezzling funds and stealing from the company for years. He had been manipulating the financial records, creating fake contracts and invoices, and diverting the funds into his own accounts. She was shocked and devastated by the betrayal, she couldn't believe that someone she trusted and considered a mentor would betray her and her father's legacy in such a way.

She immediately took action, firing the advisor and contacting the authorities to report the embezzlement. She also hired a team of forensic accountants to investigate the extent of the embezzlement, and to trace the stolen funds. But the damage had already been done, the company's finances were in ruins, and it would take a lot of time and effort to recover.

This betrayal also made her question the loyalty of those around her, she started to suspect everyone, even her closest advisors and friends. She was filled with anger and hurt, she felt that her father's legacy was being tarnished by this one person's actions. She also felt guilty for not catching the betrayal sooner, and for trusting this person in the first place.

The young woman had to find a way to move on from the betrayal and regain the trust of those around her. She knew that it would not be easy, but she was determined to make things right. She implemented stricter financial controls and oversight to prevent future embezzlement, and she reached out to the employees and customers to rebuild trust and restore the company's reputation. She also made sure to communicate transparently about the situation and the measures taken to prevent it from happening again.

But the betrayal had also taken a toll on her emotionally, she was struggling with feelings of betrayal and mistrust. She had to seek professional help to deal with her emotions and regain her trust in others. She also learned to be more cautious and less trusting of people, especially those in positions of power.

The young woman's journey as the last heir of the Wilson family had been filled with challenges and obstacles, but this betrayal had hit her hard. It was a harsh reminder of the harsh realities of the business world and the importance of being vigilant and cautious. However, it also made her more determined to succeed in her mission, to make her family's legacy one of integrity and honesty. She was determined to not let one person's actions define her or her father's legacy and she was more determined than ever to make her family's legacy a source of pride and inspiration for generations to come.

Chapter 7: The Decision

The young woman, the last heir of the Wilson family, had faced many challenges and obstacles on her journey to fulfill her responsibilities as the last heir. She had uncovered the truth about her family's history, faced betrayal from a trusted advisor, and struggled to regain the trust of those around her.

Despite these challenges, she had made progress in turning around the family's struggling businesses and restoring the family's reputation. However, she faced one final decision that would determine whether she would fulfill the conditions of her father's will and inherit the fortune.

The decision was whether to sell or keep the family's largest and most profitable business, a major oil and gas company. The company had been a significant source of the family's wealth and influence for generations, but it had also been a source of controversy and criticism due to its environmental impact and ethical concerns. The company had been accused of violating environmental regulations, and the local community had been protesting against the company's activities.

The young woman knew that this decision would have a significant impact on her future and the future of the family's legacy. She weighed the pros and cons of each option, consulted with her advisors and experts in the field, and considered the opinions of her family members and the community. She also weighed the financial implications of the decision, and the impact it would have on the company's employees and their families.

After much deliberation, the young woman made her decision. She decided to sell the oil and gas company and invest the proceeds in renewable energy and sustainable technology. She knew that this decision would not be popular with some members of her family and some of the employees, but she believed that it was the right thing to do for the future of the family, the community, and the planet.

The young woman knew that this decision would not be easy, but she was determined to see it through. She knew that this decision would have a significant impact on the family's wealth and influence, but she believed that it would also bring positive change and make a difference in the community. She also knew that it would be a difficult transition for the employees and their families, but she was committed to help them find new opportunities and support them through the transition.

The young woman's journey as the last heir of the Wilson family had been filled with challenges and obstacles, but she had faced them head on and made the difficult decision. She had fulfilled the conditions of her father's will, and had inherited the fortune, but more importantly, she had honored her father's wishes and her ancestors' legacy by making a decision that would benefit the future. She had proven herself to be a responsible and capable leader, and was ready to continue her journey as the last heir of the Wilson family.

Chapter 8: The Confrontation

The young woman, the last heir of the Wilson family, had made a bold decision to sell the family's largest and most profitable business, a major oil and gas company, and invest the proceeds in renewable energy and sustainable technology. This decision was not popular with all members of her family and some of the employees, and she knew that she would have to face the consequences.

As the young woman began to implement her plans, she was met with resistance from some of her family members, who were opposed to the sale of the oil and gas company. They believed that the company was a vital source of the family's wealth and influence, and that selling it would ruin the family's legacy. They also felt that the young woman was not competent enough to handle such a big decision.

The young woman knew that she would have to confront her family members and convince them of the wisdom of her decision. She prepared herself for the confrontation, gathering all the facts and figures to support her case. She also sought advice from her advisors and experts in the field. She also made sure to have a solid plan for the transition of the employees and their families from the oil and gas industry to the renewable energy industry.

The confrontation took place during a family meeting, where the young woman presented her plans and the reasons behind her decision. She explained the environmental and ethical concerns surrounding the oil and gas industry, and the financial benefits of investing in renewable energy and sustainable technology. She also highlighted the potential for creating new jobs and opportunities in the community and how the decision is a step towards a more sustainable future.

However, her family members were not easily convinced. They argued that the sale of the oil and gas company would ruin the family's reputation and that the renewable energy industry was too uncertain and risky. They also questioned her competence and experience in making such a big decision. The argument became heated, and tempers flared.

The young woman stood her ground, refusing to back down from her decision. She reminded her family members of the conditions of her father's will, and the importance of preserving the family's legacy in a way that was true to her values. She also reminded them of the negative impact the oil and gas company had had on the community and the environment. She also presented her solid plan for the transition of the employees and their families, and how it will benefit everyone in the long run.

In the end, the young woman's determination and conviction won over her family members. They saw the wisdom of her decision and agreed to support her plans. The confrontation had been difficult, but the young woman had emerged victorious. She had stood up for what she believed in, and had convinced her family to support her vision for the future.

The young woman's journey as the last heir of the Wilson family had been filled with challenges and obstacles, but she had faced them head on and emerged victorious. She had made the difficult decision and stood up for what she believed in. She had proven herself to be a responsible, competent and capable leader, and was ready to continue her journey as the last heir of the Wilson family.

Chapter 9: The Consequences

The young woman, the last heir of the Wilson family, had made a bold decision to sell the family's largest and most profitable business, a major oil and gas company, and invest the proceeds in renewable energy and sustainable technology. This decision had come with its own set of consequences, both good and bad.

On the positive side, the young woman's decision had helped to position the family as a leader in the renewable energy and sustainable technology industry. The investments made in these areas had begun to bear fruit, and the family's reputation had begun to recover. The community also benefited from the new jobs and opportunities created by the investments in renewable energy and sustainable technology.

However, the decision had also had its negative consequences. The sale of the oil and gas company had resulted in a significant loss of wealth for the family, and some of the family members were still resentful of the decision. The employees who had worked at the oil and gas company had also struggled to find new jobs and adjust to the change.

The young woman had also received backlash from some members of the community who had been dependent on the oil and gas company for their livelihoods. She had to deal with protests and criticism from these groups, as well as attempts to sabotage her new ventures.

The young woman knew that she had to face the consequences of her decision and she was prepared to do so. She had made sure to have a solid plan for the transition of the employees and their families from the oil and gas industry to the renewable energy industry. She also reached out to the community, explaining the rationale behind her decision and the benefits it would bring in the long term. She also worked to provide support and assistance to those who had been affected by the sale of the oil and gas company, such as offering job training and placement services.

Despite these efforts, the young woman still faced challenges in dealing with the consequences of her decision. Some family members were still bitter and resentful, and the community was not fully on board with the changes. The young woman had to work hard to maintain her reputation and win over the support of those who were opposed to her decision.

The young woman also had to contend with the financial consequences of her decision. The loss of wealth from the sale of the oil and gas company had affected the family's lifestyle and influence, and she had to make difficult choices to make ends meet. She also had to ensure that her new ventures were financially viable and that the family's fortune was being invested wisely.

Overall, the young woman's decision to sell the oil and gas company and invest in renewable energy and sustainable technology had come with its own set of consequences. Some were positive, some were negative, but the young woman had learned to accept them and move forward. She knew that her decision was the right one for the future of the family, the community and the planet. She had proven herself to be a responsible and capable leader, and was ready to continue her journey as the last heir of the Wilson family.

Chapter 10: The Regret

The young woman, the last heir of the Wilson family, had made a bold decision to sell the family's largest and most profitable business, a major oil and gas company, and invest the proceeds in renewable energy and sustainable technology. While she had believed that this decision was the right one, it had come with its own set of consequences, some of which she had not fully anticipated.

As the young woman began to see the full impact of her decision, she started to feel a sense of regret. She began to question if she had made the right choice, if she had been too hasty in her decision-making and if she had truly understood the ramifications of her actions.

The young woman felt regret for the loss of wealth and status that her family had suffered as a result of the sale of the oil and gas company. She felt regret for the employees and their families who had been impacted by the transition to the renewable energy industry. She also felt regret for the community who had been dependent on the oil and gas company for their livelihoods and were now struggling to adjust to the changes.

The young woman's regret was further compounded by the backlash and criticism she had received from some members of her family, the community, and even some of her employees. She felt guilty for not having foreseen the negative consequences of her decision and for not having done more to mitigate them.

The young woman's regret also affected her ability to move forward and make decisions for the future. She had lost her confidence and was second-guessing herself. She felt that she had let down her father and her ancestors, and had not lived up to their legacy.

The young woman knew that she had to deal with her regret and move forward. She sought the help of a therapist to work through her emotions and regain her confidence. She also made sure to communicate transparently with her family members, employees, and the community about the situation, and to take steps to address the negative consequences of her decision.

The young woman's journey as the last heir of the Wilson family had been filled with challenges and obstacles, and she had made a difficult decision that had come with its own set of consequences. She had learned a valuable lesson about the importance of considering all the potential consequences of her actions, and she was determined to use that knowledge to make better decisions in the future.

As the young woman worked through her regret and regained her confidence, she was able to focus on the positive aspects of her decision. She saw the progress that was being made in the renewable energy and sustainable technology industry, and the positive impact it was having on the community. She also saw the potential for her family's legacy to be one of leadership and responsibility, rather than just wealth and influence.

The young woman had faced her regret and had come out stronger. She knew that her decision had not been easy, but she believed that it was the right one. She had proven herself to be a responsible and capable leader, and was ready to continue her journey as the last heir of the Wilson family, with the lessons learned from her regret guiding her every step of the way.

Chapter 11: The Turning Point

The young woman, the last heir of the Wilson family, had faced many challenges and obstacles on her journey as the last heir. She had made a difficult decision to sell the family's largest and most profitable business, a major oil and gas company, and invest the proceeds in renewable energy and sustainable technology. This decision had come with its own set of consequences, some of which she had not fully anticipated, including a sense of regret and loss of confidence.

However, despite these challenges, the young woman had remained determined to see her vision for the future through. She had worked hard to address the negative consequences of her decision and to regain her confidence. She had also continued to make progress in turning around the family's struggling businesses and restoring the family's reputation.

It was at this point that the young woman's journey as the last heir took a turning point. A major opportunity presented itself in the form of a government contract to build a large-scale renewable energy project, specifically a wind farm. This project would not only provide significant financial benefits for the family, but also have a positive impact on the community and the environment by providing clean energy and reducing carbon emissions.

The young woman seized this opportunity and threw herself into the project. She worked tirelessly to put together a winning proposal, drawing on her experience and knowledge of the renewable energy industry. She also reached out to the community to gain their support and to address any concerns they had. She held meetings and town hall sessions to discuss the benefits and addressed the concerns of the local residents, farmers, and other stakeholders in the project.

The young woman's hard work paid off, and her proposal was accepted. The project was a turning point for the young woman, as it marked a significant achievement in her journey as the last heir, showing that her vision for the family and the community was valid and sustainable. The project was also a turning point for the family, as it marked a new direction and a new legacy for the family's future.

The young woman's journey as the last heir of the Wilson family had been filled with challenges and obstacles, but she had faced them head on and emerged victorious. She had made difficult decisions, faced regret and loss of confidence, but she had never given up on her vision for the future. She had proven herself to be a responsible, capable and determined leader, and was ready to continue her journey as the last heir of the Wilson family, with this project as a symbol of her success, and a brighter future for the community.

Chapter 12: The Discovery

The young woman, the last heir of the Wilson family, had faced many challenges and obstacles on her journey as the last heir. She had made a difficult decision to sell the family's largest and most profitable business, a major oil and gas company, and invest the proceeds in renewable energy and sustainable technology. This decision had come with its own set of consequences, but it had also led to a significant turning point for the family and the community.

As the young woman continued to work on the large-scale renewable energy project, she made a discovery that would change the course of her journey as the last heir.

During the construction of the wind farm, the young woman stumbled upon an old diary belonging to her great-grandfather, who was one of the original founders of the oil and gas company. As she read the diary, she discovered that her great-grandfather had always had doubts about the morality and sustainability of the oil and gas industry, and had even been considering transitioning the company to renewable energy before his untimely death. He had also written about his concerns for the impact of the oil and gas industry on the environment and the future of the planet.

The young woman was shocked and moved by this discovery. She realized that her great-grandfather had shared her vision for a sustainable future, and that her decision to sell the oil and gas company and invest in renewable energy was not only the right decision, but also a continuation of the family's true legacy. She felt a sense of pride and connection to her great-grandfather and his vision for the family and the world.

The young woman's discovery also had a profound effect on her relationship with her family members. Some of them, who had been opposed to her decision to sell the oil and gas company, were now able to see the wisdom of her actions and the importance of preserving the family's true legacy. They acknowledged their past mistakes and apologized for not having supported her earlier.

The young woman's discovery also brought her a sense of closure and peace. She no longer felt guilty for her decision to sell the oil and gas company, and was able to move forward with confidence and determination. She felt that her great-grandfather's spirit was with her, guiding and supporting her in her journey as the last heir.

The young woman's journey as the last heir of the Wilson family had been filled with challenges and obstacles, but she had faced them head on and emerged victorious. She had discovered the true legacy of her family and had honored it in her decision. She had proven herself to be a responsible, capable and determined leader, and was ready to continue her journey as the last heir of the Wilson family, with this discovery as a source of inspiration, guidance, and a sense of belonging to her family's heritage.

Chapter 13: The Plan

The young woman, the last heir of the Wilson family, had made a difficult decision to sell the family's largest and most profitable business, a major oil and gas company, and invest the proceeds in renewable energy and sustainable technology. This decision had come with its own set of consequences, but it had also led to a significant turning point for the family and the community. With the discovery of her great-grandfather's vision for the family and the world, she had found a renewed sense of purpose and direction.

With the successful completion of the large-scale renewable energy project, the young woman was determined to continue on this path of sustainability and responsibility. She knew that her journey as the last heir would not be easy, but she was determined to see it through.

To that end, the young woman began to develop a comprehensive plan for the family's future. She knew that the family's wealth and influence had always been built on the back of the oil and gas company, and that it would take time and effort to transition to a new, sustainable source of income.

The young woman's plan began with a thorough analysis of the family's current assets and businesses. She identified those that had the potential to be transitioned to renewable energy or sustainable technology, and those that could be sold or divested.

She also identified new business opportunities in the renewable energy and sustainable technology sectors, such as solar and wind power, energy storage systems and electric vehicles. She began to explore potential partnerships and investments in these areas.

The young woman also recognized the importance of community engagement and support in achieving her vision for the future. She began to actively engage with the community, hosting town hall meetings and workshops to discuss her plans and gather feedback. She also worked to establish a community development fund, to provide support and assistance to those who had been affected by the sale of the oil and gas company. This included job training programs, education scholarships, and grants for small businesses.

In addition to the financial and community aspects, the young woman also included environmental initiatives in her plan. She set targets for reducing the family's carbon footprint and promoting sustainable practices in all of the family's businesses and operations. This included investing in energy-efficient technologies, promoting recycling and waste reduction, and preserving natural habitats and biodiversity.

The young woman's plan was ambitious and would take time to implement, but she was determined to see it through. She knew that her journey as the last heir of the Wilson family would be challenging, but with her plan in place, she felt confident that she could guide the family towards a sustainable future that would benefit not only the family but also the community and the environment.

The young woman presented her plan to the family, and they agreed to support her and her vision. They knew that this would be a long-term and challenging process, but they were ready to work together to build a better future for the family and the community. With the support of her family, the young woman was ready to embark on the next phase of her journey as the last heir of the Wilson family.

Chapter 14: The Execution

The young woman, the last heir of the Wilson family, had developed a comprehensive plan for the family's future, with the goal of transitioning to a sustainable and responsible source of income. She had presented the plan to her family, who had agreed to support her and her vision. With the plan in place, it was time for the young woman to begin the execution phase of her journey as the last heir.

The young woman knew that the execution of her plan would not be easy, and that it would take time and effort to achieve her goals. She also knew that there would be obstacles and challenges along the way, but she was determined to see her plan through.

The first step in the execution of the plan was to divest the family's remaining assets and businesses in the oil and gas industry. This was a difficult decision, as it would mean the loss of significant revenue for the family. However, the young woman was determined to stay true to her vision for a sustainable future.

The young woman then began to explore new business opportunities in the renewable energy and sustainable technology sectors. She formed partnerships with companies and organizations that shared her vision, and invested in new technologies and projects that would help to promote a sustainable future.

The young woman also made sure to keep the community informed and engaged in the execution of her plan. She held regular meetings and workshops to discuss the progress of her plan and to gather feedback from the community. She also made sure to provide support and assistance to those who had been affected by the sale of the oil and gas company, through the community development fund.

The young woman also made sure to implement environmental initiatives as part of her plan. She set targets for reducing the family's carbon footprint and promoting sustainable practices in all of the family's businesses and operations. This included investing in energy-efficient technologies, promoting recycling and waste reduction, and preserving natural habitats and biodiversity.

The execution of the young woman's plan was not without its challenges, but she was determined to see it through. She knew that her journey as the last heir of the Wilson family would be challenging, but with her plan in place, and her family's support, she felt confident that she could guide the family towards a sustainable future.

Chapter 15: The Conclusion

The young woman, the last heir of the Wilson family, had embarked on a journey to guide the family towards a sustainable future. She had inherited the responsibility of leading the family after the passing of her father, who had built a vast empire in the oil and gas industry. However, the young woman had a different vision for the future, one that would benefit not only the family but also the community and the environment.

The young woman had spent months researching and studying the various options available to her before she finally came up with a comprehensive plan for the family's future. She knew that divesting the family's remaining assets and businesses in the oil and gas industry would be a difficult decision, but she was determined to stay true to her vision for a sustainable future. The young woman also knew that it would take time and effort to achieve her goals, but she was willing to do whatever it takes to see her plan through.

The young woman began the execution phase of her plan by divesting the family's remaining assets and businesses in the oil and gas industry. This decision was met with resistance from some members of the family, who were not ready to let go of the significant revenue that the oil and gas industry had been providing for the family. However, the young woman was determined to stay true to her vision, and she knew that this decision was necessary for the family's future.

With the family's remaining assets and businesses in the oil and gas industry divested, the young woman began to explore new business opportunities in the renewable energy and sustainable technology sectors. She formed partnerships with companies and organizations that shared her vision, and invested in new technologies and projects that would help to promote a sustainable future. The young woman also made sure to keep the community informed and engaged in the execution of her plan. She held regular meetings and workshops to discuss the progress of her plan and to gather feedback from the community.

The young woman also made sure to provide support and assistance to those who had been affected by the sale of the oil and gas company. She established a community development fund, which provided job training programs, education scholarships, and grants for small businesses to help the affected community members to transition to new careers and businesses.

The young woman's plan also had a positive impact on the environment. She set targets for reducing the family's carbon footprint and promoting sustainable practices in all of the family's businesses and operations. This included investing in energy-efficient technologies, promoting recycling and waste reduction, and preserving natural habitats and biodiversity.

The young woman's journey as the last heir of the Wilson family had been challenging, but it had also been incredibly rewarding. Despite the obstacles she faced and the resistance from some members of the family, she had successfully guided the family towards a sustainable future. The young woman's plan had not only ensured the financial stability of the family for generations to come, but it had also made a positive impact on the community and the environment.

The young woman's legacy lived on as the family business became a leading player in the renewable energy and sustainable technology sectors, and the community development fund continued to support and assist those in need. The family's reputation as socially responsible and environmentally friendly business had also gained recognition both locally and internationally.

The young woman's decision to take a stand and follow her vision had not only benefited her family but also the society at large. Her story serves as an inspiration for others to strive for a sustainable future and to make a positive impact on their community and the environment.

As the young woman looked back on her journey, she felt a sense of pride and accomplishment. She knew that her father would have been proud of her, and that the future of the family was in good hands. The young woman had proven that with determination, vision, and a commitment to social and environmental responsibility, it is possible to build a better future for all.

About the Publisher

Accepting manuscripts in the most categories. We love to help people get their words available to the world.

Revival Waves of Glory focus is to provide more options to be published. We do traditional paperbacks, hardcovers, audio books and ebooks all over the world. A traditional royalty-based publisher that offers self-publishing options, Revival Waves provides a very author friendly and transparent publishing process, with President Bill Vincent involved in the full process of your book. Send us your manuscript and we will contact you as soon as possible.

Contact: Bill Vincent at rwgpublishing@yahoo.com

